PENGUIN BOOKS

"Well, there's your problem."

Raised in Mount Vernon, New York, Edward Koren attended school in New York City and received his B.A. from Columbia College. He then went on to Paris, where he studied printmaking at the famous Atelier 17 of S. W. Hayter. During his early college years Koren was already beginning to work as a cartoonist, contributing to various campus publications. His work became increasingly popular, and in 1960 he began to contribute almost exclusively to *The New Yorker*. Since 1964, Koren has been teaching at Brown University, where he is now adjunct associate professor of art. *Are You Happy?* and *Do You Want to Talk about It?* are earlier collections of his cartoons. He has also illustrated a number of books, including *Pasta and Noodles* by Merry White (published by Penguin Books) and several for children. His work has appeared in numerous group exhibitions, and he has had four one-man shows.

"Well, there's your problem."

CARTOONS BY EDWARD KOREN

PENGUIN BOOKS

For Nat and Sasha

Penguin Books Ltd, Harmondsworth,
Middlesex, England
Penguin Books, 625 Madison Avenue,
New York, New York 10022, U.S.A.
Penguin Books Australia Ltd, Ringwood,
Victoria, Australia
Penguin Books Canada Limited, 2801 John Street,
Markham, Ontario, Canada L3R 1B4
Penguin Books (N.Z.) Ltd, 182–190 Wairau Road,
Auckland 10, New Zealand

First published in the United States of America by
Pantheon Books 1980
First published in Canada by
Random House of Canada Limited 1980
Published in Penguin Books 1981

LIBRARY OF CONGRESS CATALOGING IN PUBLICATION DATA
Koren, Edward.
"Well, there's your problem."
1. American wit and humor, Pictorial. I. Title.
NC1429.K62A4   1981   741.5′973   81-5195
ISBN 0 14 00.5967 9   AACR2

Printed in the United States of America by
Capital City Press, Inc., Montpelier, Vermont
Set in Linotype Bodoni Book

"He loves to be petted."

"Ah! It's the Woodwind family!"

"I love to be alive. It's fun."

"I'm sorry, I can't cope with that now!"

"When they talked about the cultural scene out here, they never told me about you."

HISTORIC HOUSE

FROM 1953 to 1961, LARRY PANE LIVED AND WORKED HERE WRITING SOME OF TELEVISION'S MOST CELEBRATED COMMERCIALS, INCLUDING THE NATSO SPAGHETTI SPOT AND THE FAMOUS SASHA BIRD FOOD CAMPAIGN

"*When the children have all grown up, we hope to move back to the city.*"

"Sweetie, will you help me with my tie?"

"Just to set the record straight, I'm leaving you because you never turn your body to the net, because you don't have a smooth swing, and because your forehand, backhand, and volley are inadequate!"

"Oh, excuse me! I thought you were somebody I know."

"Our philosophy here at Dandelion Motors is to treat the total car."

"We got a complaint that his steak au poivre was dry and overcooked, his chicken vinaigrette was prepared poorly in a sticky sweet-and-sour onion sauce that bordered on the inedible, and his leaf-spinach-with-mushroom salad was crudely seasoned."

"It shrank."

"And what do you do to maintain your cardiovascular fitness, Miss Holt?"

"You're terribly cute for someone who's fortyish."

"I have the honor to present the man who has done so much to popularize this instrument."

"Morris knows how to fix his own car."

"*The reason you all are becoming extinct is that you can't take a joke.*"

"Let us defer to the judgment of our oenologist."

"Alexandra, you possess a very large talent."

"The people who admire and appreciate you are on this side, and the ones who don't care so much for you are on the other."

"*What are you in the mood for?*"

"I'm a fresh-vegetable fan."

"I can never get it straight. Was William Carlos Williams the doctor or the insurance man?"

"Are you someone in authority?"

"Take it all off."

"It's me—Mr. Rhythm himself!"

"We still can't decide whether she's more a Hillary or an Allison."

"Good morning, Mr. Dolman. In for your twelve-thousand-mile checkup?"

"*Rick Hoffman, six miles a day, I'd like you to meet Brent Evans, ten miles a day.*"

"Excuse me. What is the name of that dish?"

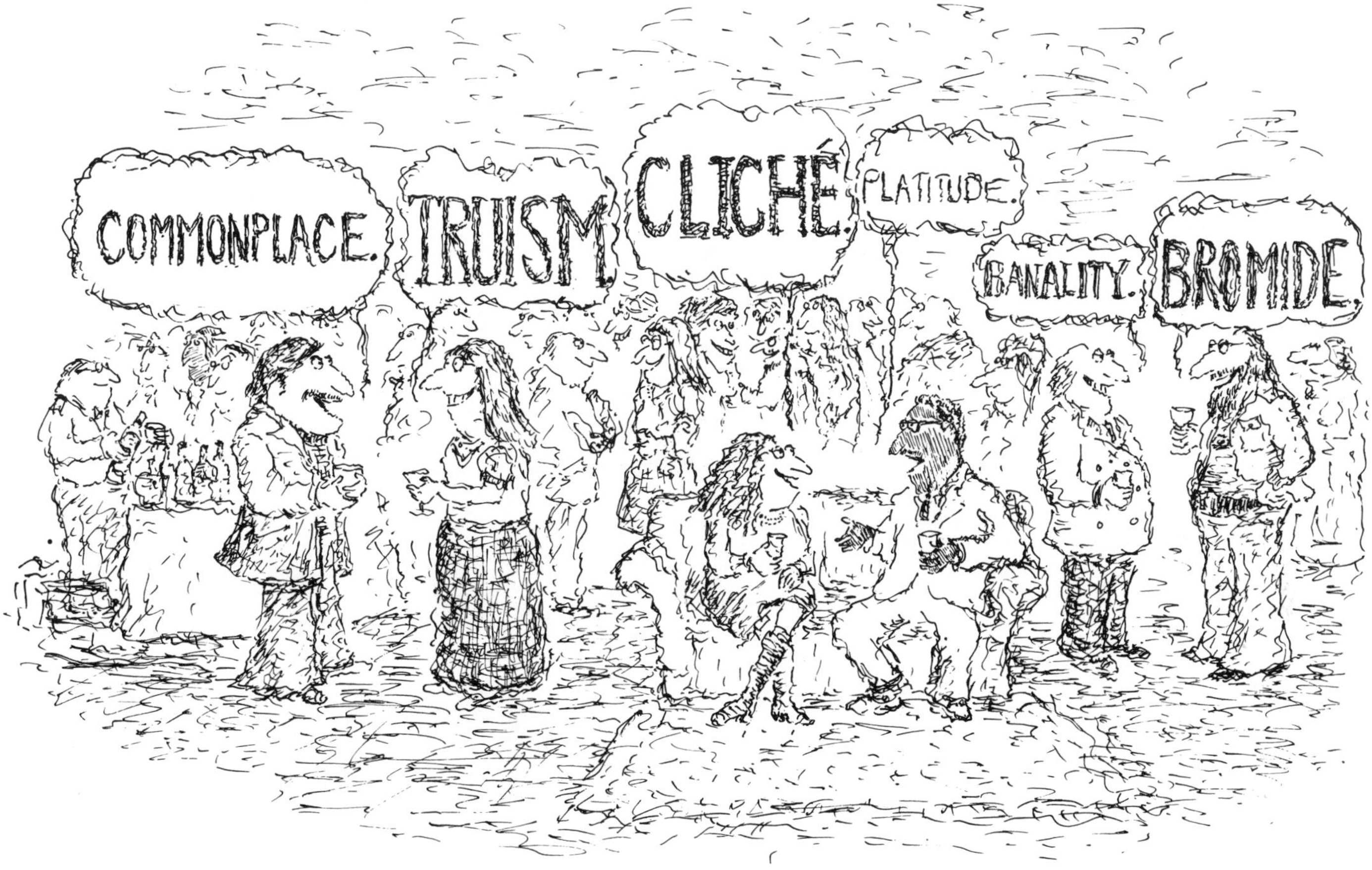
COMMONPLACE.
TRUISM
CLICHÉ.
PLATITUDE.
BANALITY.
BROMIDE.

"I fell in love with you the first time I heard your message on the answering machine."

"This is an outrage to the cooking public!"

"How long have you and Charlie been together?"

"Good morning. Kirk, Kirk, Kirk & Kirk."

"Here we are, Stephen—ready to party."

"*Do you, Jane, and you, Jonathan, jointly vow to split the royalties, paperback rights, book-club proceeds, and movie options with each other in the event that the marriage dissolves and results in a work of fiction or nonfiction based on this union?*"

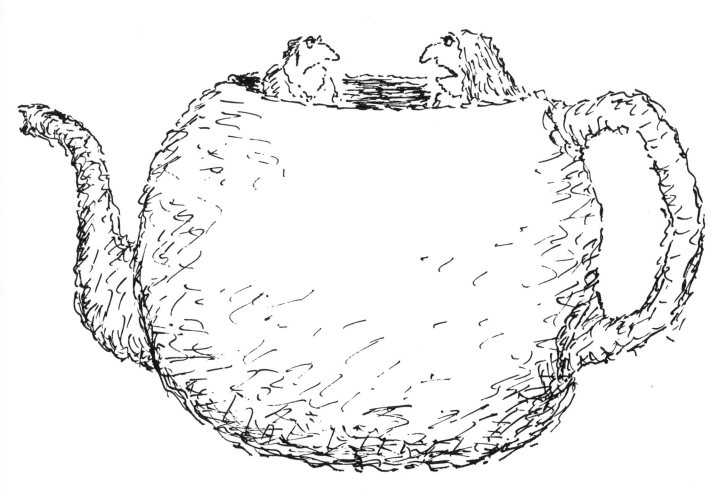

"If you don't like the tempest, get out of the teapot."

"I think it's wonderful to be so direct with your anger."

"This is an imaginative new concept in the use of leisure time."

"See anyone you know?"

"It may be presumptuous of me, but I would like to undertake a summary of Peter's ideas."

*"Jerry, I'm beginning to think it's wrong that all our fun is based
on the combustion of hydrocarbons."*

"I used to think you were a Renaissance man, Michael, but now I think you're a Neanderthal."

*"Ezra, I'm not inviting you to my birthday party, because our relationship
is no longer satisfying to my needs."*

"Let's disco, you old stodge!"

"You are my grass roots."

"And this? Trash or treasure?"

"Well, for your information, I happen to love nature."

"Daniel has become indifferent to weather conditions."

"You're right, Melissa, it does need salt. And also oregano, basil, thyme, and possibly a pinch of chervil."

"This is my only New York appearance this year."

"*I love the honesty of your lyric.*"

"Pop, you've got to be more supportive of Mom and more willing to share with her the day-to-day household tasks. Mom, you have to recognize Pop's needs and be less dependent on him for your identity."

"This is my new old man."

"*Isn't it wonderful that I'm so angry at women and you're so angry at men!*"

"John and I have decided that we're sick of hearing about women and their problems."

"Nat is here with us through the gracious courtesy of Ahsas Records."

"I think what people are going to say is 'Wow!'"

"*I'm never bored! I've got my pottery, my plants, my weaving, and my man.*"

"According to the Times, I'm 'superb.'"

"Michael <u>welcomes</u> contrasting points of view."

"Come on in, Donald, and reacquaint yourself with the meaning of fun."

"*The woman who ordered the poulet chasseur would like to come in and rap about it.*"

"No, Philip, it's not just me. We're _all_ incredibly angry!"

"I'd like you to meet our friend the protein."

"This is Alex, of Chicken Alex."

"*I'm sorry, I can't talk. I've got company.*"

"Hi! I'm all natural."

"Your depression is contagious."

"Oh, there's Freddie. He knows the best places to suffer."

"Wait, <u>I</u> know what's different. Your hair's curlier."

"Will you share my dream with me, Alexandra? A few acres somewhere,
a couple of sheep, a couple of goats, some chickens..."

"So this is your young man, Melissa!"

"Well, there's your problem!"

"I'd like to thank all my friends for their tremendous love and criticism."

"So <u>this</u> is the famous Sarah of the mustard-mayonnaise clam dip!"

"Would you be a dear and fetch me a toad?"

"I <u>love</u> your husband, Louise. He's very male without being macho."

"It's the most assertive thing I've ever done."

"You have a wonderful body."

"Are you dating anyone seriously?"

"We live a few miles from here in an architecturally significant former gas station."

"I know all about you and your pâté from the <u>New York Times</u>!"

"Now, this is a very new variety, which some people are having trouble relating to."

"New York is a constant nourishment for Daniel."

"The night woods
Listen attentively
To the owl's
  discourse,
While at dawn
The grosbeak
Elaborates the lightening sky
With musical significance."

"It's a look I believe in."

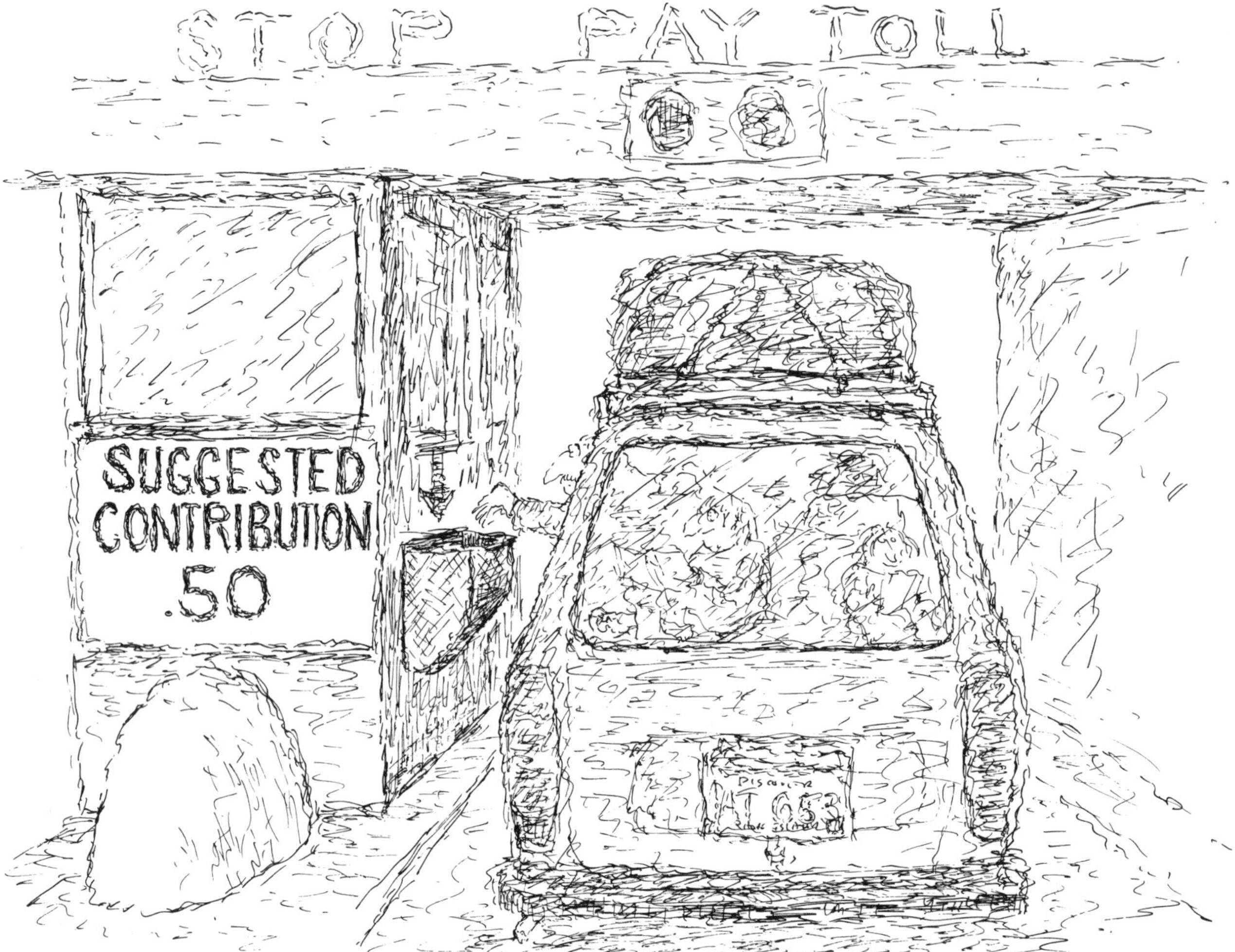
STOP PAY TOLL
SUGGESTED CONTRIBUTION
.50

"Spain—overrated. France—overrated. Switzerland! Germany!
Belgium! England! Italy! All overrated!"

"We're semi-frantic today."

"Well, I see that our time is just about up."